GREETINGS, EARTHLINGS!

DISCARD

Space Poems

by Brian Moses and James Carter

Illustrated by Chris Garbutt

AN CHILDREN'S BOOKS

First published 2009 by Macmillan Children's Books
a division of Macmillan Publishers Limited
20 New Wharf Road, London N1 9RR
Basingstoke and Oxford
Associated companies throughout the world
www.panmacmillan.com

ISBN 978-0-330-47174-9

Text copyright © Brian Moses and James Carter 2009
Illustrations copyright © Chris Garbutt 2009

3 5 7 9 8 6 4 2

A CIP catalogue record for this book is available from
the British Library.

Printed and bound in the UK by CPI Mackays, Chatham ME5 8TD

Contents

The Moon Speaks

I, the moon,
would like it known – I
never follow people home. I
simply do not have the time. And
neither do I ever shine. For what you
often see at night is me reflecting solar
light. And I'm not *cheese*! No, none of
these: no mozzarellas, cheddars, bries. All
you'll find here – if you please – are my
dusty, empty seas. And cows do not
jump over me. Now that is simply
lunacy! You used to come and
visit me. Oh do return,
I'm lonely, see.

James Carter

Moonwalker's Diary

Today I walked upon the sand
and not just of another land

A different world, a unique place
and right out here in deepest space

My steps were light, my feet took flight
in sandy seas in sun so bright

About the moon – what can I say?
It's dull and drab and dry and grey

A ball of blue was in the sky
and causing me to nearly cry

And calling me to come back home
and urging me to leave this stone

The greatest thing I've seen all day?
Our little earth, so far away

James Carter

Moon Tourist

I want to be the first Moon tourist,
I want to book a trip to the Moon,
reach deep into my pocket
for a seat on a rocket
and I hope that it happens soon.

I want to be the first to take photos
and show them off to my mates.
'See me here by the Sea
of Tranquility,
take a look at my weightless state.'

I want to be the first to buy souvenirs
like rock with 'The Moon' written through it.
A mint flavoured stick
for my children to lick
and a taste of space as they chew it.

I want to be the first to tip moondust
out of my shoes when I'm back
and to have enough
of such valuable stuff
to sell it off by the pack.

I want to be the first Moon tourist,
I want to book a trip to the Moon,
reach deep into my pocket
for a seat on a rocket
and I hope that it happens soon.

Brian Moses

Space Dog

She must have been someone's pet,
sometime before the scientists
found her, tagged and labelled her
suitable for space.
She had, someone said,
a trusting face.

She must have been shocked
when the ones she'd trusted
strapped her down
in some strange contraption,
stroked her head, tickled
under her chin, then left
and locked her in.

She must have been cowed
by the rocket's power,
shaken by the roar, the thrust
must have left her
shivering, with no one there
to calm her down
when she needed it most.

She must have whined
for a long time, while wires
taped to her skin
relayed her reactions.

She must have thought
it was some sort of game
gone painfully wrong
and that very soon they'd
release her.

She must have closed her eyes
when the temperature rose.
I hope she was thinking of fields,
of running through forests.

And if only they'd had the means
to bring her back,
she would have given them
her usual welcome,
forgiven them too,
like dogs forgive all humans
the hurtful things they do.

Brian Moses

Little Traveller
(for Gaby)

July 1969:
while the earth
is mesmerized by the moon
and eagerly awaiting
those
    first
        few
            steps

you are in your own
                weightless world
you are in your own
                timeless space
innocent of anything
other than the loving heartbeat
of your own mother ship
and gradually preparing
for your own big adventure
on this strange
                and exotic planet

James Carter

The Moonwalkers

One was Neil and one was Buzz
their tiny steps caused quite a fuss

Yet when they went up there that day
perhaps they took the spell away

For what was once a mystic pearl
is now a crusty, barren world

And did we really have to see
them walk the moon on our TV?

Well maybe no – but maybe yes
for evolution says progress

Them astronauts just did their best
so nice one, Neil and Buzz . . . I guess

James Carter

Rocket-Watching Party

*(Jaycee Beach was the nearest beach to Cape
Canaveral – later renamed Cape Kennedy – where
rockets were launched. In the 1950s there were
regular rocket-watching parties along the beach.)*

There's a rocket-watching party
at the beach tonight
and we'll cheer the rocket
till it's way out of sight.

Bring something to eat,
bring burgers and Coke,
bring binoculars
for the first sign of smoke.

We'll pick up driftwood
from along the shore,
build up a fire
as we wait for the roar,

for the whoosh of flame
that grows higher and higher

reaching to the heavens
in a trail of fire.

And we'll tremble with excitement
or maybe fear
as it blusters skywards
then disappears.

And all of us want to be
rocket engineers,
pilots or scientists,
space pioneers.

But sometimes we wait
and we wait and wait
and nothing happens
and it's getting late.

Till a message comes through,
no launch tonight,
countdown's called off,
it just didn't go right.

Then it's another night
on Jaycee Beach
when the stars still seem
so far out of reach.

Brian Moses

Dear Yuri

Dear Yuri, I remember you,
the man with the funny name
who the Russians sent into space,
were you desperate for fame?

There surely must have been safer ways
to get into the history books,
perhaps you couldn't rock like Elvis
or you hadn't got James Dean's looks.

Perhaps you couldn't fight like Ali
or make a political speech
so they packed you into a spaceship
and sent you out of Earth's reach.

And, Yuri, what was it like
to be way out there in space,
the first to break free of Earth's gravity
and look down on the human race?

I'd been doing my maths all morning,
and at lunchtime I heard what you'd done.
I told everyone back at school
how you'd travelled towards the sun.

And, Yuri, I wanted to say
that I remember your flight,
I remember your name, Gagarin,
and the newsreel pictures that night.

And you must have pep-talked others
when they took off into the blue.
I've forgotten their names but, Yuri,
I'll always remember you.

Brian Moses

That Nice Mr Armstrong

*('I remember that nice Mr Armstrong' – lady
interviewed about her memories of the Moon
Landing.)*

We were waiting for that nice Mr Armstrong
to step out on to the Moon,
and for those of us watching TV
it really couldn't come soon enough.
We thought he'd be leaping out of the ship,
but instead that nice Mr Armstrong
took his time, made us wait
for hours until the door opened
to reveal his cocoon-like shape
descending the ladder.

Long gone midnight it was, as teary-eyed I watched
that nice Mr Armstrong do his one small step
but one big leap routine, and I remember
feeling quite disappointed that
there was no one there to meet him,
no one to pop out of a crater
and say, 'Greetings, Earthlings.'

Instead it was Buzz and
that nice Mr Armstrong all alone,
as if they'd arrived at some party
that was long since over.

And I watched them leap
up and down on the moon
like crazy kids on a trampoline,
bouncing their words back home.

And after all it was
the Greatest Show Not on Earth.
It made me glow with pride,
and we all know we'll remember
that nice Mr Armstrong
and how he took every one of us
that little bit nearer
the Moon.

Brian Moses

The Moon Landing
(July 1969)

To celebrate
the first moonwalk
I invented
my own TV

All it took
was a cardboard box
some bottle tops
a spot of glue
and a piece of card –
on which I drew
an orange moon
with a tiny astronaut man
on top

Nearly everyone
came round
our house
on the big day

And the whole world
seemed to stop breathing
for a moment
as we watched
those fuzzy pictures

and listened
to those crackly voices
travelling thousands
of miles
from the moon
into our home

In fact
my aunty
reckoned my TV
was even better
than watching
the real thing –
so she put it
in the window
so everyone passing
could see
my paper moon

James Carter

Meeting an Astronaut
(Science Museum – half-term – October 2007)

He stands there proudly
  in his NASA spacesuit
    in front of
      his lunar module

He tells us
 of moonwalking
  and earthgazing
  and of the silence
    and the stillness
      and the strangeness
        of space

He confesses
  that a little bit of him
    is still
      drifting around
        up there
          in that
            big black nothing

But the module
 is only a model
  and the astronaut
   only an actor –

playing his part –
  saying his lines
    time after time after time

Yet still
  we walk away
    all starry-eyed

James Carter

To the Moon

It has been just the luck of a privileged few
to walk on the moon and look back at the view,
to stare at the planet they left behind
and to wonder if anything else they could find
would ever be quite so breathtaking as this,
no fast car ride, no daughter's kiss
could ever come close to this mountain top,
this pinnacle, this unearthly drop.

And then after the tears and the interviews
and the general hullabaloo,
and the hundreds of times you walk through the door
to talk on TV and describe what you saw,
the realization still hits far too soon,
what do you do now you've been to the Moon?

Brian Moses

Do the Space Walk

*(Remember those old fifties dance crazes? No? Well,
your grandparents will . . . go and ask them.)*

*Do wah do wah
  do be do,
do wah do wah
  do be do.*

Just fit your feet
to the prints in the dust,
swing your hips and
give it some thrust.

If you do it too slow
you'll be left behind
when it's one big leap
for all mankind . . .

Do the space walk,
don't just talk,
get up and do it,
do the space walk.

*Do wah do wah
  do be do,
do wah do wah
  do be do.*

You can walk with Buzz,
you can walk with Neil,
each of them asking
just how you feel

to be pioneers
in this new dance craze,
for once you start
you'll be doing it for days.

Do the space walk,
don't just talk,
get up and do it,
do the space walk . . .

In space, there's so much of it,
you'll never run out of space,

you can move where you like, you can twist and glide,
there's plenty of space all over the place.

Do wah do wah
  do be do,
do wah do wah
  do be do.

Do the space walk,
don't just talk,
get up and do it,
do the space walk.

Do the space walk,
take a walk outside,
do the space walk
on the wildest side,
do the space walk,
keep moving your feet,
do the space walk
to that crazy beat.
Do the space . . . . walk,
do the space . . . . walk,

one more time
let's go . . . ooooooooooooo.

Brian Moses

The First Shopping Trolley on Mars

There's all sorts of junk dumped in space,
floating about past the stars,
but through my telescope I thought I glimpsed
the first shopping trolley on Mars.

And I'd like to know which supermarket
was careless enough to allow
one of their trolleys to travel so far
that they can't recover it now . . .

Surely they must have noticed
someone strange inside their store,
an alien in the supermarket
is something you just can't ignore.

Who allowed it through the checkout?
A cashier must have taken a guess
that this was no real alien
but someone in fancy dress.

Did no one notice a spaceship
parked among all the cars,
or hear the ROAR of its engines
as it blasted back to Mars?

If aliens are coming down to Earth
to do their weekly shop
then surely this is something
that the government ought to stop.

They need to make a statement
in Parliament quite soon,
or stacks of abandoned trolleys
could be littering the Moon.

Brian Moses

It's got so much **S**pace

It's my kind of **P**lace

It's totally – utterly – cosmically **A**ce

There really is no pla**C**e . . .

like spac**E**

!

James Carter

Evidently:

Aliens

Rarely

Travel

Here

!

James Carter

See

All

Those

Ultra-cool

Rings?

Now that's what I call BLING!

!!

James Carter

What Am I?
(a cosmic kenning)

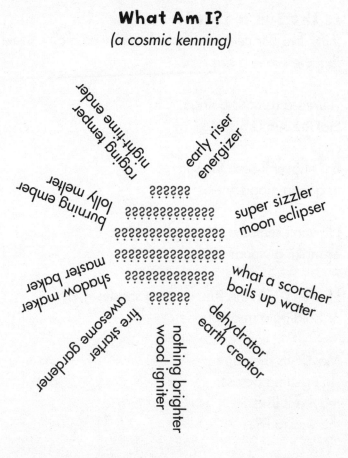

early riser
energizer

raging temper
night-time ender

burning ember
lolly melter

super sizzler
moon eclipser

shadow maker
master baker

what a scorcher
boils up water

fire starter
awesome gardener

dehydrator
earth creator

nothing brighter
wood igniter

??????
??????????????
??????????????????
??????????????????
??????????????
??????

James Carter

Is the Sun a Star?

(Fifty-five per cent of people interviewed didn't know that the sun is a star.)

There's a rumour going round
that the sun is a star,

but I haven't seen the sun
in gossip magazines.

I haven't seen the sun on chat shows
or making videos.

I haven't seen the sun wearing shades
or holding a microphone.

Maybe its message
isn't getting across,
maybe it uses
the wrong PR.

If the sun is a star,
then why don't we see it
waving from the back
of a stretch limousine?

Is it star of the stage
or star of the screen?

Does it moonwalk daily
across the sky?

Does it drop-kick a ball
through the gates of heaven?

There's a rumour going round
that the sun is a star,

but that's one rumour
too far . . .

Brian Moses

The Journey's End

What once
tore through the universe
white hot
star bright
and angry as hell

now lies broken
cold, defeated
and occasionally polished
in a glass case
marked
'Meteorites and other
space rocks'.

James Carter

What Stars Are

Stars are not
  the shards of glass
    smashed by the gods in anger.

Neither are they
  the sparkling souls
    of intergalactic travellers.

They're not even
  the blinking eyes
    of invisible skywatchers.

No.
    Stars
          are
              stars.

The dying embers
  of ancient fires
    that will never know
      how they dazzle
      and delight us
          with the final flickers
          of their lives.

James Carter

The Northern Lights

                              are not
                                    what
                                        they seem.

Not fireworks
from another realm.

Not portals
into mystic dreams.

Not cosmic curtains, or even
swarms of magic dust.

No. They're simply
solar particles
brought to us
on wild winds
bursting forth
in winter skies
like gifts
to soothe
our tired eyes.

James Carter

Simply Starlight

Observe the universe:
the expanse of space

and consider your place in it all.
And though you are small

like a star, you are light,
adrift in your life

priceless and precious
brief and unique

and this is your time
to shine.

James Carter

My Sort of Place

It's my sort of place, space,
empty and quiet, no crowds.
No one shouting out loud at night
while I'm trying to sleep.
Not a peep from Pluto
too far away to be heard anyway.
Yes, it's my sort of place, space.

I could live there quietly,
keep myself to myself,
knowing that no one would be dropping round
unexpectedly for tea,
or to tell me something I didn't want to know.
It's not an 'in your face' sort of place,
but it's my sort of place, space.

Brian Moses

The Man in the Moon

Wouldn't it be
really great
to be the Man in the Moon's
best mate?
Then once or twice
in a lunar month
you could call around
for breakfast or brunch.

Then stay maybe
and talk to his wife,
to learn about their kids
and their lunar life.
To send messages
to each other through space.
To make him laugh
and light up his face.

And wouldn't it be
really great too,
if the Man in the Moon
could call on you?
Could teach you facts
about night and day,
could watch you act
in your school play.

Could jog with you
as you run to school,
could float with you
in the swimming pool.

While all your friends
wanted autographs,
the newspapers
wanted photographs.
And everyone thinking
how really great
to be the Man in the Moon's
best mate.

Brian Moses

Love You More

Do I love you
to the moon and back?
No I love you
more than that

I love you to the desert sands
the mountains, stars
the planets and

I love you to the deepest sea
and deeper still
through history

Before beyond I love you then
I love you now
I'll love you when

The sun's gone out
the moon's gone home
and all the stars are fully grown

When I no longer say these words
I'll give them to the wind, the birds
so that they will still be heard

I love you

James Carter

A Plea to Pluto

(On 24 August 2006, astronomers all over the world voted that Pluto should be downgraded to a 'dwarf planet' due to its tiny size. So here's a poem to cheer Pluto up after receiving that tragic and indeed deeply upsetting news.)

Pluto, don't be doom and gloom.
Yes, you're smaller than the Moon.

But has there ever been so nice
a teeny-weeny ball of ice?

And hey, you're still a planet true.
A diddy one. So don't be blue.

I care not what they say you are . . .
Pluto – you're a little 'star'!

James Carter

Advice for UFO Spotters on the Extraterrestrial Highway

(The Extraterrestrial Highway runs close to the mysterious Area 51 in Nevada, where rumour has it that the American government is trying to make contact with aliens. UFO spotters regularly gather on the ET Highway in the hope of seeing alien craft.)

1. Don't forget to take the essential UFO-spotters' special kit: a pen and notebook, a pair of binoculars, a camera, *The Observer's Book of Spaceships* (New Edition) and *How to Speak Conversational Plutonian in Two Days.*

2. If you meet an alien by the side of the road, trying to thumb a lift and doing the old 'Take me to your leader' routine, don't do it. It's a very long drive from Nevada to the White House and, besides, what on earth would you find to talk about along the way?

3. If an alien suggests to you that you go back to its spaceship for jelly and cake, be warned. You may find that you have become a prize exhibit in an alien's collection of objects to be removed from Earth and taken back home!

4. Aliens come in all shapes and forms but if you suddenly see a black and white object with orange flashing lights approaching you from behind, that's probably not an alien and more likely to be the highway police.

5. If the police ask you what you are doing so close to Area 51, tell them you're birdwatchers.

6. If you do meet an ET and it asks to borrow your mobile phone to call home, don't let it. The cost of the call will be astronomical.

7. Same with your pocket calculator: that alien might just want to turn it into a highly dangerous human-brain-frazzling contraption. So beware.

8. We know you know this, but most aliens are space tourists. They will be keen to see some culture doing their short visit. Try a spot of country dancing or even singing them some of your favourite space songs: 'Reach for the Stars', 'Is This the Way to Asteroid XYO?' and the all-time classic, 'What's That Coming Out of the Sky, Is It a Bird, Is It a Plane, or Is It Really a Long Cigar-shaped Object Flying at an Impossible Speed?'

9. If you do get to see a UFO, don't be too disappointed if no one believes you!

10. Keep a silver frisbee in the back of the car in case you don't get a picture of the real thing.

Brian and James

The Alien Eye/The London Eye

Only you and only I
know this wonderful wheel
is not what it seems
but the stuff of sci-fi,
the cause of bad dreams.
It's an alien eye
dropped from the sky,
the fabulous eye
of a being, all-seeing,
a hypnotist
who has tricked us all
to believing what he
would have us believe.
Like a gift from the Greeks
we have dragged it inside,
this pride of London,
this fabulous eye . . .

And we will queue
to board the eye,
till one day soon
this alien eye
will take off smoothly
into the sky
in the biggest
alien abduction
ever . . .

Dare you ride it?

Brian Moses

Aliens Stole My Underpants

To understand the ways
of alien beings is hard,
and I've never worked it out
why they landed in my backyard.

And I've always wondered why
on their journey from the stars,
these aliens stole my underpants
and took them back to Mars.

They came on a Monday night
when the weekend wash had been done,
pegged out on the line
to be dried by the morning sun.

Mrs Driver from next door
was a witness at the scene
when aliens snatched my underpants –
I'm glad that they were clean!

It seems they were quite choosy
as nothing else was taken.
Do aliens wear underpants
or were they just mistaken?

I think I have a theory
as to what they wanted them for,
they needed to block off a draught
blowing in through the spacecraft door.

Or maybe some Mars museum
wanted items brought back from space.
Just think, my pair of Y-fronts
displayed in their own glass case.

And on the label beneath
would be written where they got 'em
and how such funny underwear
once covered an earthling's bottom!

Brian Moses

Little Green Men

I just don't know what to do
about all these little green men,
they follow me into town and then
they follow me home again.
I find them queuing at the bus stop
or waiting to catch a train,
these groups of little green men,
all of them looking the same.

They queue with me in the post office,
buying stamps for strange-sounding places,
their little green grins fixed permanently
upon their little green faces.

I think these little green men
must be on a special mission,
but I just can't shake them off –
I'm too far out of condition.
They run with me when I run,
always keeping me in sight.
They glow really bright in the dark,
so I can't escape them at night.

My stress levels and my patience
are really being tested.
I ought to phone the police
and have them all arrested.

But it makes no difference at all
if I rave or if I rant,
once little green men stole
my underpants,

now it looks like they're back
for me.

Brian Moses

The ET Runway

*(It is rumoured that in the Nevada Desert in America
there is a specially prepared ET Runway with
welcome messages permanently beamed into the sky
to attract the attention of low-flying extraterrestrials.
Meanwhile, in a back garden in Sussex . . .)*

We've laid out what looks like a landing strip
in the hope of attracting an alien ship
and we've even managed to rig up a light
that will flash on and off throughout the night.
And we've spelled out 'welcome' in small white
    stones
and we've messed around with two mobile phones
till now they bleep almost continuously
and their signal plays havoc with next-door's TV.
But it's for the greater good of mankind,
this could be a really important find.

And we're going to have an interstellar fun day
when aliens land on *our* ET runway.
What a day it will be and what a surprise
when alien spacecraft snowflake the skies,
when strange beings christen our welcoming mat
to gasps of amazement, 'Just look at that!'
And to anyone out there listening in
the reception we'll give you is genuine.

We promise there'll be no limousines
to take you to tea with kings and queens.
No boring politicians from different lands,
no chatting on chat shows or shaking of hands,
no scientists waiting to whisk you off
to investigate every bleep, grunt or cough.
It will only be us, just me and Pete
and a few friends from school you'll be happy to
    meet.
We could interview you for the school magazine:
'Does your spacecraft run on gasoline?'

And we know it's not the desert in Nevada,
but we really couldn't have tried much harder.
So if you can hear us, please make yourself known,
send us a signal, pick up the phone.
We've seen you out there, effortlessly gliding,
introduce yourselves now, it's time to stop hiding.

Brian Moses

Abducted by Aliens

When Jack came back to school
after one day's absence, unexplained,
he went and told his teacher
he'd been abducted by aliens.
She told him not to be so daft,
but he gave us all the details –
what the spacecraft had looked like,
how extraterrestrials kidnapped him
then carried him on to their ship.
And Jack told his story
again and again. 'When they landed,' he said,
'I was terrified, couldn't move,
I nearly died, then a blade of light
cut the night in two, trapped me
in its beam so I couldn't see. I felt
arms that were rubbery wrapped around me
like the coils of our garden hose.
And I don't recall anything more
till I found myself back on the ground
while rasping voices were telling me
that everything I saw they would see,
that everything I heard they would hear,
that everything I ate they would taste.
And I know they're out there watching me
in some intergalactic laboratory,
I'm a subject for investigation,

constantly sending back information,
a bleep that bleeps on a bank of screens,
abducted by aliens, tagged and then freed.'

'What nonsense you talk,' his teacher said.
'Take out your books, who's ready for maths?'
But Jack couldn't make his figures come right.
If communication works both ways, he thought,
then he might benefit too –
maybe aliens could help solve his multiplication!

Brian Moses

A Helicopter. Maybe

It's getting dark
and we're walking
down the hill
past the park
and you point
at the sky
and you say
'Hey. What's that?'

'What? What's what?'
I say and
then I see

a little craft
with rows of
coloured flashing lights
whizzing slowly across
the night sky.

It hovers awhile
then gradually returns
back to where
it came from.

'Wow!' I say
'UFO!'

You go quiet.

Without a word
you dash off
down the hill
all the way
to your house.

We never talk
about it again.

What was it?

James Carter

Aliens Report on Planet Earth

Strange sounds from Planet Earth
are upsetting all our frequencies,
disturbing our cosmic nerves,
interrupting flying sequences.

The high-pitched whine of chainsaws
makes my tentacles quiver,
the constant thud of steam hammers
is shaking up my liver.

The awful roar of their primitive planes
makes my three heads ache,
the incessant rumble of traffic
keeps me permanently awake.

My ears are very sensitive
to even the slightest vibrations
from the twanging of guitar strings
to a pendulum's oscillations.

Their washing machines drive me wild
with their irritating clatter,
and I wish I could bury their mobile phones
to quieten their pointless chatter.

We'd best get back to the depths of space,
where there's no noisy trouble or fuss.
We've checked out this planet and now know for sure
it's no earthly use to us!

Brian Moses

Space Fact: There is no sound in space. There is no
air for sound to travel through outside the Earth's
atmosphere. This is why astronauts need spacesuits
and oxygen tanks.

The Littlest Things

Be careful.

Be careful because
the littlest things
can have
the biggest consequences.

A single beat
of a butterfly's wing
may be enough
to trigger an earth tremor
or a tidal wave.

So imagine what
a cross word
or a slammed door
or even a mean thought
could spark off
out in space –

it could
unhinge the moon
or anger the sun
or bring on
a colossal comet.

Just be careful.

James Carter

Remembering Thea

Thea
they say
in the time
before time
you were
Earth's sister planet

Thea
they say
that you died
and disintegrated
when you collided
with Earth

Thea they say
that by doing so
you gave our world
its extra gravity
its atmosphere
and even our moon

Thea
I say
how strange it is
that when
the letters

of your name
t – h – e – a
are rearranged
e – a – t – h
they nearly spell . . .

James Carter

Your Star

I read somewhere
that you can now buy
your very own star.
Seriously.
A star you can call
your very own –
one you could point at
in the night sky
and say –
'Hey, look!
There's my star!
Over there – no,
not the really big one –

that little twinkler
next to it.
See?
There. That's mine,
that is.'

Yet unlike a football
you can't play with it.

Unlike a mate
you can't ring it up for a chat.

Unlike a nice old lady
you can't go and visit it.

Unlike a pet
you can't pick it up
stroke it – cuddle it – and say to it
'Hewwo 'ickle fluffy fing.'

But you can give it a name
peer at it through a fancy-pantsy telescope
smile at it
and – hey, if no one's around –
you can even
have a little wave at it.

James Carter

Elvis Is Back

(Rumours persist in the press that the rock singer Elvis Presley faked his death. One of the most bizarre ideas is that Elvis was in touch with aliens and that they came down to Earth to spirit him away! One day, of course, he may decide to make a comeback!)

When aliens brought Elvis Presley back
it looked as if we were under attack
as a mother ship of incredible size
sank down to Earth right in front of our eyes,
and it really gave us an almighty shock
when out of its doors stepped the King of Rock.

There was laughter, tears and celebration,
Elvis is back, he's been on vacation.
There he stood looking leaner and fitter,
Elvis is back, in a suit made of glitter.
It seems the doubters were right all along,
Elvis is back with a dozen new songs.

He's been cutting an album somewhere in space,
now he's bringing it home to the human race.
And the world is listening, holding its breath,
to recordings of Elvis made after his 'death'.

And of course he'd duped us all into thinking
it was pills and burgers and too much drinking
that killed him off, but that wasn't the case,
Elvis escaped to a different place.
He's been touring out there, a star upon stars,
rocking the universe, Venus to Mars.

And as alien ships descend from above
we're sending out our message of love
and hoping they'll show no desire to attack,
but we don't really care because ELVIS IS BACK!

Brian Moses

In the Future

In the future
will we zip between planets
just as swiftly and easily
as we nip to the supermarket
or the filling station?

You could have breakfast on Mercury,
lunch on Jupiter
and in the evening be wined and dined
in a charming Italian pizza parlour
on Pluto.

You could zoom around the Galaxy
pressing time switches,
calling in at whatever planet took your fancy,
with satellite connections bringing you
universal mail (or umail).

How fantastic would that be
speeding down the Milky Way
looking out for space cameras past Saturn
in case they flashed you?

Nobody wants an interplanetary speed ticket
with points on their licence
keeping them earthbound.

The garden centres of Mars,
the bars of Jupiter,
the nightclubs of Neptune,
all benefiting from this interstellar flit
through the time zones
and then . . .

at the flick of a switch or the press of a button
(depending on which model of time machine
you're tripping in . . .)
you can be back home
for the latest episode of
your favourite space soap.

Now doesn't that sound
out of this world?

Brian Moses

Last Time

Leaving Earth for the last time,
we're locking all the doors.
We're leaving the planet to fend for itself
now it's bruised and broken and sore.

The silence here is unreal
now that everything's shut down.
No noise from traffic or factories,
quietness covers each town.

No time for tears or regrets,
we just didn't listen enough.
The message was stark and clear,
the solution far too tough.

We hoped the scientists were wrong,
that they couldn't predict our fate.
We put off paying attention
until it was far too late.

The last spaceships are leaving now,
there's nothing more to be done.
No one can survive any more
beneath this scalding sun.

It's a strange and awful feeling
to be leaving the land of your birth,
maybe someday someone will find
a way to recycle the Earth.

Brian Moses

Space Station 215

This is Space Station 215
letting you know that we're still alive
and kicking, out here at Planet Rock
with DJ Robot, your Cosmic Jock.

We're bringing you these sounds from space,
sounds that will take you to some other place.
We got Androids, Humanoids, Starlighters too,
We got Moondog and Big Star, just for you.

We got a shipload of sounds comin' in today,
flying them fast along the Milky Way.
We got R & B, we got rock 'n' roll,
we got the strangest sounds from a deep black hole.

We got Mercury Rev, we got Moontrekkers too,
We got Sigue Sigue Sputnik comin' to you.
We got all sorts of music to give you a lift,
we're rockin' so hard we'll make your planet shift.

So listen in and listen good
to these sounds we bring to your neighbourhood.
Just turn your radio up to the sky,
we're blasting down from way up high.

This is Space Station 215
letting you know that we're still alive
and kicking, out here at Planet Rock
with DJ Robot, your Cosmic Jock.

Brian Moses

Visiting Jupiter

There must be some celestial M25
all the way to Jupiter,
or how else can you explain
why it takes six years to get there?
Six years without a service station on the way.
Six years of stopping and starting
and travelling through roadworks,
single carriageway all the way to Venus.
And what would it be like for any spaceman
travelling there?
'Just slipping out to visit Jupiter,
see you soon, don't wait up . . .'
Not much scope for holidays either,
no possibilities of day trips or weekend breaks.
Six years!
What are you doing for the next six years?
Think of all the books you could read,
the games you could play – not I spy though,
'I spy with my little eye something beginning
with S . . . yes, SPACE,
lots of it,
how did you guess?'

Brian Moses

It Came from Outer Space!

It did. Oh yes, and at a guess
it came from far away
from some unheard-of galaxy
beyond the Milky Way

It landed in your classroom
while you were tucked in bed
by 8 a.m. next morning
it was talking to the Head

And now it is your teacher.
'Ah-ha!' you say. 'That's why
Miss acts so very strangely
she fell out of the sky!'

James Carter

Is Your Teacher an Alien?

(Not sure? Well, here's some top tips on spotting extraterrestrials.)

When she answers her mobile:
Does she say things like, 'Hello, darling. I'll be home by six. Don't forget to put the baked potatoes in the oven.' Or is it something more like, 'Greetings, Commander Greebleblubb. The earthling children are performing well. I will begin experiments on their tiny little brains this afternoon.'

When she goes home:
Does she a) catch the bus, b) drive her car, or c) pretend to walk home but actually dash round the corner, jump into her spacecraft, yell, 'REACH FOR THE STARS!' and whizz off into the sky?

In the classroom cupboard:
Is there a) normal stuff like pencils and paper, or b) loads of weirdo stuff like jam jars containing human eyeballs?

When she does assemblies:
Does she come out with the usual, 'Well, children, today I want to talk to you all about caring and sharing. Do you know what that means, children, do you? Do you? Or does she let slip with stuff like, 'Right then, young earthlings, if you are not prepared to cooperate with us Jupiterians, our next school trip will be to the sun. Yes, THE SUN – that very hot thing in the sky. And that includes you too, Year 6. So stop smirking.'

What does she look like:
Fairly human and normal? Or when you get up really close can you see that she has three tongues? And do her fingertips glow in the dark? Are her toenails really microchips recording your every thought, breath and action?

Take a sneaky peek in the staffroom at breaktime:
Is your teacher a) flopped out on a chair drinking gallons of coffee and dunking some nice cookies, or is she b) ripping off her human costume, jumping out of the window screaming . . .

I'm
AN
A l i E N –
GEt ME
oUt Of hERE
! ! ! ! ! ! ! ! ! ! !

James Carter

Behind the STAFF ROOM door

the very best of BRiaN MoseS

This brilliant book is packed with old friends – including 'What Teachers Wear in Bed', 'Shopping Trolley' and 'Walking with My Iguana' – and introduces us to some wonderful new poems too.

from 'Behind the Staffroom Door'

Ten tired teachers slumped in the staffroom at playtime,
one collapsed when the coffee ran out, then there were nine.

Nine tired teachers making lists of things they hate,
one remembered playground duty, then there were eight.

taking out the Tigers

Poems by Brian Moses

from 'Taking Out the Tigers'

At twilight time
or early morning
a tiger-sized ROAR
is a fearsome warning
as a huge cat swaggers
through a fine sea mist,
its paws the size
of a boxer's fist,
when they're
taking out the tigers
on Sandown beach.

In this fantastic collection of poems Brian Moses tells us – in his inimitable style – about tigers, teachers, witches, angels, conkers, football, aliens, dinosaurs and hang-gliding over active volcanoes!

THERE'S A HAMSTER IN THE FAST LANE

Poems chosen by Brian Moses

Illustrated by Jan McCafferty

Here is the craziest collection of animal poems EVER!

Get ready to meet a tortoise on a trampoline (boing!), a cat who bites back (ouch) and a poor little rich dog (whimper). You'll find out what all the fashionable ferrets are wearing at the moment – and how your average cat reacts to being served the wrong brand of cat food. MIAOW!

WILD!

Rhymes That Roar

Chosen by James Carter and Graham Denton

Want to go WILD?

We've got all kinds of curious critters prowling around in this book, from minibeasts to massive beasties – in poems, fact pages and quizzes galore!

BUG HUG

Hey
little
bug – how
gimme a hug! do you hug – *gimme a hug!*
or cuddle or kiss
your mum or sis –
gimme a hug! with all those arms *gimme a hug!*
and legs and things –
and wiggly bits and
wobbly wings? For
gimme a hug! however hairy or *gimme a hug!*
creepy or scary
even the ugliest
bug needs
a HUG!

James Carter

A selected list of titles available from Macmillan Children's Books

The prices shown below are correct at the time of going to press. However, Macmillan Publishers reserves the right to show new retail prices on covers, which may differ from those previously advertised.

Behind the Staffroom Door

The Very Best of Brian Moses   978-0-330-01541-8   £4.99

Taking Out the Tigers

Poems by Brian Moses   978-0-330-41797-6   £3.99

There's a Hamster in the Fast Lane

Poems chosen by Brian Moses   978-0-330-44423-1   £3.99

Wild! Rhymes That Roar

Chosen by James Carter and Graham Denton   978-0-330-46341-6   £4.99

All Pan Macmillan titles can be ordered from our website, www.panmacmillan.com, or from your local bookshop and are also available by post from:

Bookpost, PO Box 29, Douglas, Isle of Man IM99 1BQ

Credit cards accepted. For details:
Telephone: 01624 677237
Fax: 01624 670923
Email: bookshop@enterprise.net
www.bookpost.co.uk

Free postage and packing in the United Kingdom